SONGBIRD

NANCY

JOURNEY
FORTH™

Greenville, South Carolina

Library of Congress Cataloging-in-Publication Data
Lohr, Nancy.
   Songbird / Nancy Lohr ; illustrated by Johanna Berg.
      p. cm.
   Summary: When his father is imprisioned and faces death for
maiming in a foundry accident, Truxton proves his love for his
parent whose fate is in God's hands.
   ISBN 1-57924-297-9
   [1. Fathers and sons—Fiction. 2. Family life—Fiction. 3.
Christian life—Fiction.] I. Berg, Johanna, ill. II. Title.

PZ7. L82895 So 2000
[Fic]—dc21   99-048423

Songbird

Project edited by Debbie L. Parker
Designed by Miin Ng
Cover and illustrations by Johanna Berg

© 2000 Journey Books
Published by Bob Jones University Press
Greenville, South Carolina 29614

ISBN 1-57924-297-9

15 14 13 12 11 10 9 8 7 6 5 4

Dedicated
to the memory
of this nation's godly ancestors

"In chariots some put confidence,
some horses trust upon:
But we remember will the name
of our Lord God alone."

Psalm 20:7
from the *Psalms of David in metre*

Contents

Terms

Botetourt (bŏt' ŭ tŏt) governor of Williamsburg from 1768 to 1770

gaol (jāl) a prison where a guilty person awaited his judgment

gentry (jĕn' trē) upper-class people who were both wealthy and socially important

middling sort (mĭd' lĭng sort) lower-class laboring people who had little wealth or social importance

pewter (pyo͞o' tər) a silver-colored metal used for common utensils and dishes

Psalter (sôl' tər) a small book containing David's Psalms written in poetic form

shire reeve (shīr rēv) an officer who enforced the law

skep (skĕp) a handwoven beehive shaped like a dome and set on the ground in a garden

unguent (ŭng' gwənt) a soothing ointment

Chapter One
The Tyrant

Truxton Pilcher lay belly to the earth and arm out-stretched. A small dark seed rested on the tip of his finger. "Come little chick, come." His voice was barely a whisper as he willed the small bird to him.

The little creature viewed him cautiously but did not move away. With a steady hand Truxton held the seed below the flat red beak. The crested head sank ever so slightly, and in a flash the seed was gone. Truxton's finger was as still as a stone.

SONGBIRD

The tiny bird raised its beak to swallow. Then it fixed its shiny black eyes on Truxton. He in turn studied the odd curve of the auburn wing. The chick took a single hop nearer his outstretched finger. He closed his hands around the little bird. There was no struggle.

Truxton wriggled backwards. The low branches bit into his back, and the smell of the dirt tickled his nose. Behind him, his younger sister Elizabeth chattered happily.

He pulled his head out from under the hedge. Elizabeth bounced on her toes. The sunlight here in Mother's kitchen garden made her fair curls almost red.

"Did you catch it, Truxton?" she asked.

"I did that, but he allowed it, gave himself up. Look, Elizabeth. His wing is bad. Be still now."

He pulled his thumb back a tiny bit to look in at the bird. Elizabeth's breath was warm on his arm. "What kind is it?" she asked.

"You tell me, Elizabeth. Look at the markings—black head and red crest, brick red wings and a white breast. Father says you can know any man or beast by his markings."

Elizabeth took a long look at the little bird. "I don't know how you do it, Truxton." She sighed. "So many birds, and you know them all. They just look like birds to me."

"More's the pity. This one is called 'The Tyrant.' It's in the Catesby book." Truxton raised his hands and examined the little chick. It nested quietly, and the delicate white feathers rose gently with each breath. "Tyrant. A fine name for our King, little fellow, but not for you. That bad wing has taken every bit of fight from you."

Suddenly Elizabeth spun around and announced loudly, "Mother, Truxton caught another bird, and this one has a broken wing."

Mother gathered up the corners of her heavily laden apron and stood up. "Is that so?" She kicked the hem of her billowing skirt out from underfoot and stepped across the garden rows in strong, full strides. "Then I'd say the bird chose a fine place for his mishap. He'll find none better than Truxton to patch him up. Give me a look, son."

He lifted his hands to show her the bird cupped within. "A Tyrant, Mother, and a chick at that."

"Beautiful colors. How bad is the wing, do you think?"

"It's not broken through. That whippoorwill last spring was far worse. See there—the soft curve? If he'll let me straighten the wing, a splint will hold it steady until the bone knits."

"My poor dear Truxton," Mother said. "Your hands are far better suited to birds than bellows."

"Noble and Charles are already smiths," said Elizabeth. "Does Father need all three?"

"Indeed he does, Elizabeth." Mother shifted the load of potatoes in her apron. "It takes much labor to form pewter goods. We of the middling sort must all toil if we are to succeed here in Williamsburg."

Toil, Truxton thought. *Always toil.*

Elizabeth didn't listen to Mother's answer. She was talking to the little bird.

Mother looked over the hedge that bounded the garden. Truxton had often seen her stop her work and gaze into the woods behind the Foundry. She spoke quietly, almost to herself. "I suppose it is a rare man who walks a path of his own choosing." She was thoughtful for a moment. "But back to work now." She hoisted her heavy apron.

"I need your help with these potatoes, Elizabeth. Truxton, you may tend your patient, then get back to your chores in the Foundry."

The heavy skirts moved away. "Alone at last," he said aloud. He looked around the garden.

His glance fell on a bee skep that lay on its side. He had helped draw out its amber honey some weeks ago. He and Elizabeth had filled glass jars for Mother and then sucked the sweetness from their fingers. Truxton licked his lips, just remembering.

On this autumn afternoon, the woven cone was empty of both bees and honey.

"This will hold you for now, little fellow." Truxton lifted the skep upright and set the tiny bird within. *Now, what for a splint? A willow branch? Yes, that will do nicely.* He snapped off a short, straight twig. Then he broke a dangling thread from the buttonhole of his breeches.

He returned to the skep and sat down beside it. "Little Tyrant?" Truxton called to the bird. "Are you ready?" When he raised the top, the little bird cocked his head. But he did not flee.

"Softly now," Truxton crooned, and he gathered up the feathered bundle. He held it snugly against his stomach with his forearm. "Let me see."

Gently, but firmly, he extended the wing to its full span. "Does that hurt?" He lay the slender twig along the length of the wing. The little bird did not fight.

"You'll be fine now." He wound the thread around the twig and between the feathers until the odd curve in the wing was straight. Truxton tied a knot, bit off the extra thread, and let out his breath.

"That's a brave little Tyrant. You will have a strong wing by and by. Let's put you in my cage."

Chapter Two
The Evening Meal

Truxton's mouth watered as he breathed in the delicious aroma. He looked at Elizabeth and whispered, "Meat pie!"

Father and Mother stood at either end of the simple pine table, and Truxton and Elizabeth, Noble and Charles stood behind their benches. He wondered whether any of them could hear the growling of his stomach.

If Father heard, he gave no notice. He began the meal as usual. "Psalm 37 verse 1, please," he said.

In unison they recited the verse from Father's Psalter:

> For evil doers fret thou not
>> thyself unquietly;
> Nor do thou envy bear to those
>> that work iniquity.

Truxton bowed his head with the rest of the family, and Father prayed. Silently Truxton said, *Thank you for my new bird.* Father's prayer went on, and Truxton finished his own prayer. *Please help its wing to heal.*

"Amen," said Father.

Truxton climbed over the top of the bench he shared with Elizabeth and seated himself. Carefully he tucked his napkin into his collar, and Mother smiled her approval. He ran his tongue around his lips, waiting for Father to fill each bowl.

When all were served, Father inquired of each about the day. Truxton ate steadily. *I wonder how old the chick is.* The deep voices of his older brothers went on. *Tomorrow I'll look for the nest—can't be far.* Noble and Charles conversed with Father about their work in the Foundry—old work finished and new work begun. *They never talk about anything but dishes and spoons.*

He felt Elizabeth hook her ankle around his, and together they swung their legs back and forth. Their bench began to squeak along in rhythm to the simple song in his mind . . . *my **Ty-rant**, my **song-bird**, my **Ty-rant**, my **songbird**.*

"Children!" Mother's voice broke into his thoughts. "Put your feet on the floor and be still." She turned to Father. "Did you know, Gyles, that the Foundry cage has a new tenant?"

Truxton loved it when Father smiled at him. Deep wrinkles fanned out from the corners of Father's eyes.

"I did not," Father said, "but I have ceased to be surprised at the regular stream of guests through Truxton's twigged inn. What this time, son?"

Truxton returned the smile. "A Tyrant, sir. A beautiful young chick. He has a broken wing." He thought about the wing. "It's not broken through, just a bad bend, and he let me straighten it. Elizabeth and I haven't looked for the nest yet—"

Father interrupted. "Take a breath now." He laughed. "You are the quietest boy I ever met until the topic turns to birds. Then you chatter like a silly girl."

Elizabeth frowned. "Governor Botetourt likes birds just as much as Truxton!"

6

"Softly now, Elizabeth." Noble leaned in toward her. "Did Father call *you* a silly girl?"

"I think not." Charles joined in the fun. "And as far as girls go, Elizabeth, you aren't so bad. I say we should keep you."

"Let's keep Truxton as well." He heard the sneer in Noble's voice. "He sweeps up a goodly amount of pewter filings from beneath our benches. That's a wretched job I'll gladly yield to the young dreamer."

"Do not fault him, Noble," said Father. "Life under this British King gives a man precious little to dream about."

Truxton clenched his spoon and muttered under his breath, "If you would but tuck the bench apron in your belt, there would be no need to clean your mess."

"Enough." Father's single word brought an uneasy silence to the table.

Chapter Three
Hard Work

The next morning, Truxton stood alone in the Foundry. With the fire warming his back in the early morning chill, he drew shapes in the dusty surface of Noble's workbench. He traced wings and beaks and birds in flight. He thought of his brothers. "I wish I could be in the woods today," he said to himself.

Reluctantly he lifted each of Noble's tools and brushed the silvery dust from the surface of the table. "Only the middling sort must reuse even their dust!" He raised the loose edge of the leather apron nailed to the bench and swept it clean. "If we were well-to-do gentry, I could sweep our dirt straight out the door." He cleaned the stool below the bench and moved it out to the grass near Tyrant's cage. The little bird chirped.

"Hello, little fellow. Finished your seeds already? I'm cleaning the Foundry this morning. 'Tis a hateful job, but Father says I must do it. He says we cannot waste the tiniest scrap of pewter."

Back inside, Truxton took up the horsehair brush and knelt again to search out more fallen bits of metal. He gently swept the surface of the grate from the outer edges inward and then lifted the grate itself from the stone floor and carried it outside. "You see, Tyrant? Not a speck of dirt or metal on this." Truxton glanced at the woods and breathed heavily. "If my chores were done, I would carry your cage into the forest."

He turned and slowly walked back inside.

He cleaned Father's bench in the same manner, then Charles's in turn.

Finally, he knelt and swept the stone floor beneath the workbenches. He was careful so that no dust filled the air. He brushed his pile of pewter filings and dirt onto a broad magnolia leaf, and the floor was clean.

Truxton carried the leaf to the sifting table and tipped it onto the screen. Then he sang aloud as he tapped the sides of the frame. "My **Ty**-rant, my **song**-bird. My **Ty**-rant, my **song**-bird."

He watched the particles of dirt fall onto a cloth below. Firelight danced on the large splinters of pewter that remained in the screen—splinters filed from spoons, rough bowls, and pipe tamps.

Truxton emptied the silvery shards into the crucible used for melting pewter. He breathed in the smoky smell of the bowl. Then taking the cloth, he stepped outside. "Look Tyrant, I'll flap my wings for you." He snapped the cloth up and down in the early morning air.

When the cloth was clean, he tucked it into the top of his knickers. He picked up a grate with one hand and a stool with the other. Then he dragged both back into the Foundry.

The sun was high in the sky when Truxton finally nestled the crucible into the coals. He spit once into the embers just to hear the hiss. Then he took up the leather bellows and squeezed the handles steadily; it blew against the embers until the glowing red coals turned white-hot.

His knuckles tingled in the heat, and his eyes burned as the shards melted into a silver pool.

Chapter Four
Goodrich Scrivner

Truxton stood at Father's elbow to watch. With the sharp point of his awl, Father traced the shape of a handle. He drew the left half in one of the sand-packed boxes before him, the right half in the other. When the mirrored shapes were finished, the two halves would be joined. Then Truxton would help pour molten pewter into the top of this channel.

"See there, Father? The top of your handle? It curves just like the Tyrant's wing. Don't you think?"

Father stopped and smiled at him. "You see birds in every design, son." With a steady hand Father hollowed out the shape of the handle. Finally, he carved the lines and curls that would decorate the finished piece. "I need your hands now, Truxton."

Truxton carefully raised his mold to face the one Father was lifting. Cautiously they slid the boxes together until the sandy surfaces met. Truxton held both boxes tight while Father bound them with a leather strap.

"What do you think, son?" Father stepped aside so that Truxton could look into the opening at the top of the mold.

A small round hole was all that he could see of Father's handle. The two sides met each other exactly.

"It is perfect, Father. I will never learn to shape a mold like you."

"You will," Father assured him. "Once you have the heart for it. Now, let's cast the handle."

With long and sturdy tongs Truxton lifted the glowing crucible from the coals. He took its measure with his eye. "Looks like I reclaimed enough to pour the whole handle, Father. It's a good thing you have me gather up what Noble and Charles drop in carelessness."

"You crow like a rooster, son," Father chided.

Truxton's cheeks burned, but not from the heat of the crucible. He set the fiery vessel on the bench.

"It *is* good to have your help, Truxton." Father raised Truxton's chin with his hand. "But you must not call your brothers careless. A craftsman thinks more about the shape he is drawing forth than that which is cast aside. The drawing and reclaiming both have their part."

"A fine speech, Pilcher." The large frame of Goodrich Scrivner filled the doorway of the Foundry, and his loud voice filled the air. "Would you were as honest with your hands as with your words."

"What is it today, sir?" Father turned to face the man. "State your business and take your leave. I've got molten pewter on the bench."

The man's broad shoulders rubbed the door frame as he strode into the Foundry. His pink brocade vest strained across his broad stomach. Truxton turned away from the flowery smell of the man's wig. He wrinkled his nose.

"You know my business; I find that you are selling yet another pair of candlesticks at Tarpley's Store." Mr. Scrivner surveyed the small Foundry. "This shop steals patrons from Scrivner's Silversmithing and gives them poor goods in the deal. You close your doors, or I'll have them closed for you."

"Pewter serves the middling class well, Scrivner, those who can ill-afford fine silver." Father's voice was steady, but the muscles tightened in his cheeks. "I've stolen no coins from your purse."

Father put great worth in being an honest man— Truxton knew that. He remembered the time Noble had found his file on Charles's bench and had called his older brother a thief. Oh, how angry Father had become. Truxton could still hear Father's words: " 'Tis the very reason I left England! To live honestly before God and man."

"No man . . ." Father took a single step closer to Goodrich Scrivner. "*No man* will call a Pilcher a thief without just cause."

Silently Truxton slipped out of the Foundry and ran to the kitchen. "Master Scrivner," he said. Mother picked up her skirts and bolted from the room.

Hurry, Mother. Truxton thought. *Faster.*

They had reached the edge of the kitchen garden when a terrible howl came from inside the Foundry. Mr. Scrivner stumbled from its dim interior. He clutched his wrist, holding up an injured hand, and cried, "I'm burned!"

Truxton stared at Mr. Scrivner's hand. Blisters formed large, ugly clusters right before his eyes. The skin turned as black as a raven's wing, and the man's face was twisted with pain.

"I'll get the unguent!" Truxton darted into the Foundry for the soothing ointment they put on burns.

"Get the boy away!" The huge man held his wounded arm out of Truxton's reach. "No child of yours will touch me, Pilcher."

Father took the man by the shoulders and forcibly sat him on a wooden bench. "Truxton *will* touch you, and you will be glad of it by and by."

The smell of scorched flesh stung Truxton's nose as he gently lifted away bits of pewter. Then he scooped out a measure of the salve and coated the wound. He looked into Master Scrivner's tortured face. "I'll need to bind this with cloth, sir, to separate your fingers."

Through clenched teeth the man spoke. "You'll do no more to me, boy." The large man twisted his shoulders out of Father's grip and stood up.

He cradled his injured hand and glared at Father. "I tell you, Pilcher." His voice was an angry whisper now. "I *can* take you before the bench for maiming, and believe me, I will." Mr. Scrivner staggered through the gate.

Chapter Five
A Silversmith's Hands

All was silent. Truxton turned to look at Father and saw that his head hung low.

"Can he do that, Gyles?" Mother said in a hushed voice. "Try you for maiming?"

"He can."

"What did you do? What happened?" Mother twisted her apron in her hands. "Truxton, leave us."

"No, he was here." Father sat on the same oak bench where Mr. Scrivner had been but a moment ago. "He should know what happened."

Truxton's head began to spin. He edged away until his back pressed against the trunk of a nearby tree. It held him upright.

The stillness was awful. *Say something, Father.* But Father just gazed at the pewter buckles on his shoes.

Finally Father spoke. "Scrivner accused me yet again, Sarah, of stealing his patrons. Threatened to close my foundry."

Father took a long breath, then he continued. "I answered as I have before. I sell good pewter. With God's help, I am an honest man." His next words were almost too quiet to hear. "Scrivner uttered an oath, Sarah. He laughed and said only a fool would pretend to serve a God no man can see."

He said slowly, "I am . . . no . . . fool."

Truxton could tell how important those words were to Father. They sounded heavy—as heavy as when Father rested his hands on Truxton's shoulders.

Mother stood at Father's side and laid her hand on his. Father raised his head and looked up at her.

"Any good man knows that, Gyles," she said. "How did he burn his hand?"

"I took his arm, to lead him from the shop . . . but he wheeled away. He lashed out at me with his other fist," Father said. "I only meant to take his arm." He clenched his hands until his knuckles turned white. Beads of sweat formed on his face.

The knot clutching Truxton's stomach was as tight as Father's fists.

"I don't know what happened next," Father said. "He must have hit the crucible. It happened so fast. The pewter ran through his fingers like . . . like water."

Father looked down at his own hands, then closed his eyes and shook his head. It seemed to Truxton that Father must be feeling the white-hot pewter in his own hands.

A sickening thought struck Truxton. "I left the crucible on the bench."

"Where it belonged, son." Father reached out his arm and beckoned Truxton to come to him. "You bear no blame. The accident happened in my foundry—*my foundry*—during an argument I should never have joined."

"But it was just that . . . an accident." Mother wrapped her hands in her apron. "Surely the judge will know that?"

Father sighed. "A silversmith's hands are his tools, Sarah. If indeed Scrivner has been maimed, he has the right to take me before the bench."

When the family gathered for dinner that evening, no one seemed to notice the savory smell of stew. Truxton's stomach churned, but it did not churn from hunger.

Father turned pages in the tiny Psalter and found the passage he sought. He raised his head and spoke quietly. "We are called upon to serve our God well, to show His goodness to those who care to see. I will read Psalm 145 verse 8:

> The Lord is very gracious,
> in him compassions flow;
> In mercy he is very great,
> and is to anger slow."

Father closed the Psalter and slipped it into his pocket. He looked at each one of them in turn and then at Mother. "I answered anger with anger today, and I am ashamed. There will certainly be a price to pay."

Then Father bowed his head. He thanked God anew for His provisions and begged His forgiveness.

A hush cushioned the meal. Truxton wrestled with thoughts far tougher than the meat upon his plate. *What will happen to Father? Oh, why didn't I set the crucible back into the coals—away from the bench?*

Chapter Six
Gaol

The next day, Truxton knelt by the small bird's cage and untied the Tyrant's splint. The bird allowed him to feel the roundness of its outstretched wing. "It's healing, little fellow."

The latch on the garden gate clicked, and Peter Pelham let himself in. "Oh, no!" Truxton whispered to the bird. "The gaoler."

The man called across the garden. "I need to speak with your father, Truxton."

"He's in the Foundry, sir." Truxton gently set the chick back inside its cage. "I'll get him."

But before he could fasten the clasp on the cage, Father stepped into the garden. "Good morning, Peter."

The two men looked long at each other.

"I'm sorry, Gyles."

"It can't be helped, Peter. 'Tis a hard business, this."

Mr. Pelham carried no chains. Truxton knew the gaoler could trust Father to come without shackles. He cried out in a voice that sounded like a stranger's. "Please, sir. Don't lock him away!"

But the gaoler's face was as hard as stone. The King's law must be obeyed.

Father squared his shoulders and followed Mr. Pelham through the gate.

Mother laid her hand on Truxton's back, but he didn't know when she had come. Elizabeth was beside Mother, silent for once. Charles and Noble stood outside the Foundry.

They all watched until Father disappeared from sight, then Mother led Elizabeth back to the house. Truxton turned to look at the Tyrant. The cage door stood open, and the little bird was gone.

Charles spoke in his deep voice. "We'll need that spilled pewter, Truxton."

"I'll help you lift it from the floor." The kind voice didn't sound like Noble.

To Truxton, the next days passed like soldiers on review, each one like all the others. His brothers did what work they could without Father's guidance. And he did his own chores without being prodded, but more than ever he wished to run deep into the woods.

Chapter Seven
Father

Each evening, Truxton and Elizabeth carried Father's meal to the Public Gaol. His sister chattered every step of the way.

On this night the gaoler turned the great key in the lock as Truxton raised his heavy basket. "Mother put in some extra soup for you tonight—for your kindness."

The gaoler lifted his candle and looked into the basket. "You carry a *book?*"

"Our Psalter, sir. Father reads to us every day."

"Is that so? I didn't know your father could read."

Mr. Pelham smoothed the collar on Truxton's jacket. "I am grateful to your mother, but give your father my soup." The gaoler handed Truxton the candle and swung the huge door open. "Mrs. Pelham is expecting me."

"Father! How are you?" Elizabeth threw her arms around him. Truxton hastily set the basket of food on Father's pallet. He held the candle at arm's length but likewise hugged Father with all his might.

"Fine, now that you are here," Father said.

"Would you say that," asked Truxton with a smile, "if we came without the food?"

Father leaned back on his pallet. "Well, now." In the dim light of the cell Father stroked the rough whiskers on his chin. Truxton knew there were wrinkles at Father's eyes. "That is a hard question for a man to answer."

"Father!" Elizabeth exclaimed. "What a horrible thing to say."

Father pulled her into his lap. "I'm teasing you, little one, just teasing." He nuzzled her hair with his face and kissed her cheek. "What more could a man ask than time with his children?"

Elizabeth took Father's face in her hands and kissed him on the tip of his nose. "That's better. Let me get your stew." She slid off Father's lap and lifted a crock from the basket. "It's rabbit stew."

"My favorite," Father said, and he reached for the spoon.

"Be quiet now, Elizabeth." Truxton held the candle's dim flame close to the tiny Psalter. "I will read today's passage to Father while he eats." Truxton read Psalm 18:28, the same verse Charles had read to them that morning.

> The Lord will light my candle so,
> that it shall shine full bright:
> The Lord my God will also make
> my darkness to be light.

"Isn't God's Word full of promise?" Father asked thoughtfully. Truxton could tell he didn't want an answer.

Father finished his stew and lifted the pewter mug of milk to his lips.

Then Elizabeth asked the same question she asked every evening. "What will happen, Father?"

And Father gave the same answer. "When the judge comes, he will hear both Mr. Scrivner and me. He will weigh the matter and give my sentence."

Tonight Truxton dared to ask his own question. "What *can* he choose, Father?"

Father looked up at him. "When you come with tomorrow's evening meal,"—Truxton could hear caution in his voice—"have Elizabeth stay to help your mother. And bring your brothers."

The next day passed slowly, and the knot in Truxton's stomach steadily tightened. He helped his brothers all afternoon but kept watch out the window at the sun overhead. Finally, when the shadows began to lengthen, each set his work aside. Truxton banked the fire and hung the bellows on the peg. Charles closed the shop.

Noble carried a crock filled with hearty potato soup, Charles held a jug of cool water, and Truxton brought another blanket to keep Father warm in autumn's chilly air.

Truxton waited impatiently while Father ate. He rocked from one boot to the other where he stood. He breathed deeply and tasted the gaol's dusty air. Finally, Father set the empty crock at Charles's feet and wiped his mouth on the back of his sleeve.

Then Father cleared his throat. "About your question, Truxton. I have talked a good deal to Peter about all of this. He knows as much about the King's law as any man in this town." Charles sat on the stone floor by Father's knee, and Noble knelt close by.

Only Truxton stood. He held the light of the flame on Father's face. "And what does he say, Father?"

Father took a deep breath. "My guilt is already settled. I am in this gaol for maiming Goodrich Scrivner. Peter says it is not likely, but the judge *could* send me away from Williamsburg to live in another colony."

Charles put his arm around Father's shoulder and opened his mouth to speak.

"But," Father continued, "most likely the judge will find my action worthy of the gallows." The cell was hushed. "That is the sentence of our King."

Truxton felt as if a horse had kicked him in the stomach.

"The judge will be in Williamsburg soon, surely before November." Father reached out and squeezed Noble's knee. "When that day comes, Noble, you must stay with Elizabeth. Keep her safely away from the court."

"Yes, Father."

"And Charles." In the dim light Charles looked as much a grown man as Father did. "I ask you to attend your mother at court. Give her strength."

Charles took Father's hand. "I will, sir."

Then Father faced Truxton. The light of the candle flickered between the two of them. "You have been a part of this from the start, Truxton. You may finish it as you choose. Either stay with Noble and Elizabeth or join your Mother and Charles."

No one spoke. No one moved.

"That is it?" Truxton was stunned. He simply could not take in what he had just heard. "The King will hang you?" His voice was loud in the small chamber.

Father drew him into his lap. Truxton had not been cradled like this for a long time, but he leaned in against his father's chest and began to cry. Father brushed the hair away from Truxton's face and murmured, "That is the King's law."

Peter Pelham's key grated in the lock. Truxton sat up and scrubbed his sleeve across his eyes. The gaoler pulled open the heavy door and reached for the candle.

They made their way home in the twilight. *The King's law.* In his mind Truxton could see the wooden gallows. He could hear a trap door fall away. *The King's law.* He could

hear the gasp of a crowd, but he would not allow himself to see Father's neck within the noose.

Elizabeth had already eaten and been tucked into bed. Mother led them to the table and filled their bowls with steaming soup. Then she gently drew from each their news.

When they were finished, she asked Truxton, "Do you have the Psalter?"

He nodded and pulled it from the pocket of the jacket he still wore.

"Turn to Psalm 86, son. Read for us verses six and seven."

Truxton turned the pages. He read first to himself the verses his mother had requested. Though he tried to clear his throat, his voice was tight and tears stung his nose.

> Hear, Lord, my pray'r; unto the voice
> of my request attend:
> In troublous times I'll call on thee;
> for thou wilt answer send.

When Mother spoke, her voice too sounded tight. "We do not know how God will answer our prayer, but this we do know: God will answer." She led them in earnest prayer, and then sent Charles and Noble to their beds in the loft. She walked Truxton to the alcove he shared with Elizabeth and helped him climb up onto his bed. As she bent over to kiss his forehead, Truxton whispered, "There must be another way."

Her soft arm brushed Truxton's face as she stroked his hair. "Nothing short of a royal pardon." She kissed him. "The Lord Himself will care for us." She turned and left the chamber.

But how? Truxton wondered. *How?*

Chapter Eight
Truxton's Plan

The Pilcher sons tried to continue their chores in the Foundry, but they talked more than they worked.

"Father dreamed of a better life in the colonies," said Charles.

"Better?" scoffed Noble. "Better when the same king rules us still?"

" 'Tis more than that. Father is master of his own shop here."

"And pays taxes on everything save the very air we breathe!"

Truxton remained silent. He sat by the hearth and traced birds in the ashes. While his brothers talked, he dreamed. He spoke not a word until he had every detail worked out. Only then did he share his plan.

"A royal pardon," said Truxton. "That's what Father needs."

"And just how do we get a royal pardon?" asked Noble.

"I will go to the Mansion and ask Governor Botetourt to pardon Father." His words held a strange certainty.

Charles turned on his stool to look at his younger brother. "That sounds like a deed already done, Truxton," he said. "How do you plan to reach the Governor?"

Truxton had rehearsed the scene so carefully in his mind that it painted itself easily before his brothers now. "The Governor thinks he can get one bird to sing the song of another."

Charles nodded. "I've heard that."

"What do birds have to do with pardons?" asked Noble.

"Just listen. I will catch a songbird."

"The only birds you catch are wounded!" Noble scoffed. "You can't catch a healthy one."

"Remember the thrush? I caught it in the basket Elizabeth and I wove."

Charles interrupted. "Let's just suppose you *could* catch a bird—what then?"

"I will take it to the Governor as a gift, and while I am there, I will ask him to pardon Father."

"Just like that?" Noble asked.

Truxton nodded. "Mother says Governor Botetourt is a fair man—a friend of the middling sort."

"And if you fail?"

"Then we have lost nothing," Truxton answered. "Please, Charles. Give me time to trap the bird. Let me try."

It was long before Charles spoke. "No one can deny that you do have a way with birds, nor that the Governor fancies them as well." He turned to Noble. "I can do my day's work alone. You?"

Noble seemed hesitant to answer. "I guess so."

"Then I suppose it cannot hurt to try."

In the dirt of the garden path Truxton sketched a familiar basket trap. It must be strong but very light so it would not crush the bird. Elizabeth watched each stroke of his stick. "Get four lengths of grapevine, Elizabeth, long enough to reach from your nose to your toes. I'll get willow branches."

Then the two began to weave the basket. Truxton bent his branches into gentle arches and pushed the ends into the dirt.

"I'll hold the tops for you," said Elizabeth. She drew the arches together, and Truxton wrapped them with the vine until the framework was secure. Then he laced the vines in and out of the branches.

"Gently, Elizabeth. You're squeezing it."

"Sorry."

Piece by piece Truxton wove the vines into the willow structure until the airy trap was done. A slender twig would raise the mouth of the basket off the ground. He would tie a string to the twig. Then he had only to tug on the string, and the sturdy basket would drop over any bird that dared walk beneath.

"A Mock-bird, Elizabeth. That is what we shall catch."

"Where?" Elizabeth's eyes danced.

Truxton chewed on his bottom lip and looked out in all directions from the garden where they stood. "I think the scrub trees near the River James would be best, Elizabeth. Are there any berries still on the vine?"

"Perhaps deep within."

Truxton carried the trap inside and returned with Mother's berry basket.

He followed Elizabeth as she ran ahead, her fair curls bouncing. "Let's try here, Truxton."

Truxton reached in through the tangled vines, and his fingers searched for each tiny berry. One by one he dropped them in the basket.

"I can't find any more," Elizabeth said. "Mother and I filled our whole basket when last we picked."

Truxton drew his hands out of the brambles. Berry juice stained his fingers, and the thorns had pricked his arms.

Truxton rocked back on his heels and looked into the basket. "Well, we need only enough for a tiny songbird. This will have to be enough."

Mother met them in the kitchen. "Charles told me of your plan, Truxton." She looked worried. "I wasn't serious when I spoke of a pardon. The Governor will not receive a boy into his mansion."

"But he might receive a bird, Mother. May I not even try?"

Elizabeth wrapped her arms around Mother's waist. "Please?"

Truxton looked into Mother's face. She had closed her eyes and she murmured, "Dear Lord, is this the path we should take?" Then she fell silent.

When Mother looked again at Truxton, she took a deep breath and said, "All right then. You may go, but you will take some bread along for yourselves; and I expect you home by the time the crickets begin their night song."

He gathered up the trap, a cloth bag, and a length of string while Mother wrapped a chunk of bread in a napkin. Then Truxton and Elizabeth hurried to the river.

Chapter Nine
The Governor's Bird

The smell of moist, warm earth reached Truxton's nose, and he slowed his pace. "Softly now, Elizabeth. Stay a bit behind me while I look for a place to set the trap."

He walked quietly through the underbrush. He moved more and more slowly, and so did she. When Truxton came to a stop, he pointed to a small clearing. There he nestled the trap into the grasses, then raised the basket on the twig. He attached the string and drew it along the ground and into the undergrowth.

That done, Truxton settled himself behind a cover of foliage and turned to Elizabeth. It was her turn. She drew a gently curving line of berries to the trap. Then she stepped back into the thicket.

A gentle breeze made the leaves rustle. Birds sang above the sound of the flowing river. Truxton strained to hear a Mock-bird's call. Elizabeth mouthed the question, "Do you hear one?"

He shook his head no.

They waited. They watched. They listened. But not a single bird ventured near their trap.

Truxton pointed at the napkin, and silently Elizabeth folded back its corners and broke the bread in half. She handed one piece to him and kept the other for herself. Long after the bread was gone, raindrops began to dance on the surface of the river. At first Truxton did not feel the rain in the leafy thicket, but as the drops continued to fall, he finally stood. "Run for home, Elizabeth." He gathered up the trap and several of the berries and followed close behind.

At breakfast the next morning Truxton said, "I'm going back to the river."

"Not today, Truxton. You are sorely needed in the Foundry." Mother looked worried. "I know how hard you boys are working, but we are still falling behind on our accounts."

Charles spoke up. "If I can finish polishing the porringer for Master Cripps, I can deliver it today."

Noble said, "I'm packing a sand mold and probably will be able to pour spoons before day's end."

Truxton knew better than to argue, but he gave Charles a pleading look.

Charles studied his younger brother. Full of determination, Truxton looked back at Charles. "Perhaps we should let him try, Mother," he said. "Surely none of us can get into the Mansion."

Mother spoke to Noble. "You cannot pour alone. Your father won't allow it."

Noble locked eyes with his brother, the brother he often badgered and mocked. "Well," Noble said reluctantly, "maybe Truxton can do what he has dreamed about. I will not pour until he's back to help."

Not another word was spoken. Truxton pushed a final bite of muffin into his mouth. He and Elizabeth quickly set out for the River James.

SONGBIRD

The tall grasses were dotted with morning dew, and raindrops hung like pearls from the leaves.

The trap was set and baited anew. The thicket closed in around Truxton and his sister, and the wait began.

Rays of sunlight cut through the branches, and sounds of the morning filled the air. Truxton cocked his head and listened for the distinctive sound of the Mock-bird. Elizabeth watched her brother's face. His slow smile was enough to tell her what his ears alone could discern. They both crouched low and fixed their eyes on the trap.

Truxton saw it first . . . the feathered head. The bird pecked the ground and then hopped forward to peck again. Soon the Mock-bird ate the first of their berries. With tantalizing slowness, the bird moved down the path of berries. It paused just beyond the rim of the trap.

Truxton waited. His fingers gripped the end of the string, and he lay still. He held his breath, his heart pounding in his ears.

Another hop, then two, and the bird was under the trap. Still Truxton did not move. He waited and then a moment more until the bird began to peck at the berries there. When the bird's head dipped low, Truxton tugged on the string and the basket fell neatly down. Elizabeth ran out of the thicket and held the basket firmly to the ground over the thrashing bird.

Truxton joined her. He began to coo softly to the bird, and in a short while the bird calmed and looked through the trap at Truxton's face.

"Hand me the bag, Elizabeth." Truxton raised the trap slightly and slid the sack underneath, bird and all. He tied the mouth of the bag closed and raised it triumphantly. "The Governor's bird, my lady."

Chapter Ten
Governor Botetourt

Back at his chores in the Foundry, Truxton could think of nothing else save gaining an audience with Governor Botetourt. He stepped outside many times to watch the Mock-bird settle into the Tyrant's little cage.

The sun had crossed its highest point when Charles stopped polishing the porringer. "Noble, let's take Truxton to Mother and ask her to allow him to go now. He's precious little help here."

The trio of boys found Mother and Elizabeth in the kitchen rolling pastry for their supper.

"Mother." Truxton spoke first. "May I go to see the Governor now, please?"

"He did catch the bird," Charles added.

Mother brushed a strand of hair back away from her face, leaving a floured streak in its place. She paused long while she looked at the three boys.

"I don't suppose I can or should stop you now, son. But mind you," Mother cautioned, "the Governor has no obligation to hold court with the children of Williamsburg."

"Yes, Mother."

She sighed. "Very well, then. Make yourself present-able, and let me see you before you go."

Charles helped wash Truxton's neck and ears—Mother would be certain to check there. Noble smoothed Truxton's hair, and Elizabeth knelt and wiped the dust from his boot tops. Truxton himself tucked his shirt in smoothly and pulled the knees of his breeches down over the tops of his stockings.

He returned to the kitchen and stood before Mother. She smiled at her youngest son, kissed the top of his head, and whispered, "Godspeed, my son."

In the garden Truxton picked up the caged Mock-bird. He looked toward the Palace Green, a place where the mid-dling sort seldom went. The bird twittered as every step brought Truxton closer to the mansion. Over and over he rehearsed his words until his feet brought him to the marble steps.

The huge brass knocker hung on the solid door above Truxton's head. He set his cage on the top step. Then standing on tiptoe, he leaned against the door and stretched high until his fingers reached the knocker. He lifted it once and let it fall. Before he could lift it a second time, the latch rattled and the door swung open.

A handsome butler stood tall in a royal red uniform. "Yes?"

Truxton was speechless before the buttons, the buckles, and the golden braiding.

The butler cleared his throat. "Well?"

"G-good day, sir," he stammered. "I am Truxton Pilcher of Williamsburg." He swallowed once. "I am here to see his Lordship."

The man's eyebrows lifted. "Truxton Pilcher of Williamsburg? And the Governor expects you?"

"Well, no, sir. He isn't exactly *expecting* me," Truxton's voice trembled. "But I think he will be grateful if you allow me in. I caught a Mock-bird for him."

Slowly the tall man smiled. "The Governor will be pleased with your kindness." He reached down with a gloved hand. "I will give him your gift."

Truxton knelt to pick up the small cage, but he did not give it to the butler. "Please, sir." His eyes met the man's. "Oh, please, sir. May I give it to the Governor myself?"

"Although the Governor enjoys the company of the Colony's children, Master Pilcher, he is not feeling well today. He is not to be disturbed." The butler's voice was firm. "I will give him your gift."

These were not the words Truxton wanted to hear.

The man spoke again. "Or should I tell the Governor to look for you on his next evening walk?"

Truxton answered the butler. "No, sir. That is the only time I can see my father . . . when I carry his food to the Public Gaol."

Truxton's heart felt as heavy as a millstone. He raised the simple cage to the butler. "You can give the bird to the Governor. But will you also tell him"—Truxton's voice cracked with emotion—"that Gyles Pilcher is a *good* man and not a fool?"

The butler studied the young boy, and then, refusing the cage, he stepped back. He allowed Truxton to enter a room lined with shining firearms and crowned with British flags. He led the boy down a corridor and stopped at a massive inlaid door.

The butler paused with his hand on the doorknob. Then he turned the knob and swung open the door. He announced, "Master Truxton Pilcher to see Governor Botetourt."

A man looked up and drew a rasping breath.

The butler simply stated, "I know your Lordship wished to rest today." He looked down at Truxton. "But the boy bears a gift. You share a common interest." Then, putting his right foot forward and bowing slightly, the man backed away.

Truxton stood wide-eyed in the splendid room. The heavy door closed behind him, and he stood facing the Governor. All words failed him.

"The name is Pilcher? Truxton Pilcher?"

Truxton swallowed and nodded.

"Of Pilcher's Foundry?"

The boy nodded again.

The Governor rubbed his forehead. "I pass it often on my evening walks." He looked at the handwoven cage and waited for the boy to speak. The man stood and walked around his desk. "Well, come. See *my* birds."

Only then did Truxton notice the gilded cages hanging on stands. He fell in beside the Governor and looked within each chamber. Beautiful birds with bright eyes looked back at him. "Do they sing, sir?"

"That they do," the Governor answered. "But I have yet to hear them trade songs." He smiled down at the boy. "I should think they would like to try another tune."

"My mother says each sings his own song best." Truxton raised the roughly woven cage. "I brought you a Mock-bird, your Lordship. Perhaps *he* can sing as you wish."

Governor Botetourt knelt in front of the cage. Man and bird studied each the other. The pale-faced man whistled a soft melody, and the Mock-bird cocked his head in answer.

Without a word, Truxton gently moved the cage toward the Governor, and the man received it silently. He carried it back to his desk. With one hand the Governor closed a

leather-bound volume and moved it to the side. In its place he set the cage.

"Young man, as a servant of England's King, I receive goods to meet man's every want or whim. This songbird, however, I will treasure as a gift from your heart."

Truxton's cheeks burned.

"But I cannot believe you caught this bird simply to satisfy my fancy." Truxton could feel the Governor's eyes. "What really brings you to my gate?"

Truxton's heart beat hard within his chest. He stood erect and gripped the sides of his breeches. "It's the accident, sir. In Father's foundry. Master Scrivner called my father a thief. Spoke an oath. Father took his arm—but only to lead him out. And the pewter spilled." Truxton swallowed hard. "I put the crucible on the bench. And now Father must die . . . for maiming." His voice trembled. "Please, Your Majesty, will you pardon my father?"

The man answered. "I am not His Royal Majesty, Master Truxton, though you honor me with your error." He paused. "I, like your father, am but a servant of England's King. I try to conduct my business with kindness and integrity as does your father. His reputation is known to me."

The Governor stood and moved to a stuffed chair by the window. He patted the seat of another chair and nodded to Truxton. "Sit."

Truxton obeyed. The Governor clasped his hands together and raised his knuckles to his chin. The room was quiet, save the sound of rustling feathers and the Governor's breath.

The man's forehead furrowed, then smoothed. He leaned forward and lowered his head until Truxton could see only the carefully powdered wig.

Finally the Governor broke the silence. "The power to pardon is mine, Master Truxton, but whether it is right to pardon your father . . . that is something I must weigh carefully." He drew a noisy breath. "I will have my men examine the matter." He rubbed his eyes. "You shall have my answer soon."

"Thank you, your Lordship."

Chapter Eleven
The Announcement

The meal around the pine table was flavored with more hope than the Pilchers had known for days. Truxton sounded like Elizabeth as he chattered about the Governor's mansion. He told them again and again how Father had looked at dinner when he learned of Truxton's bold request.

When the food was finished and the dishes were moved back, Mother opened the Psalter. "Truxton, we all thank you for the courage and resourcefulness you have shown today. Your father is proud, I know. Very soon either the judge or the Governor will determine your father's fate. But we must all remember that God rules over all. Psalm 20 verse 7 says:

> In chariots some put confidence,
>   some horses trust upon:
> But we remember will the name
>   of our Lord God alone."

"We must trust our God, even if the answer seems hard. Charles, will you pray tonight, please?"

With his eyes closed, Truxton thought Charles sounded like Father. He listened carefully as his brother implored the Lord to meet their needs and to give Father courage.

SONGBIRD

A sudden clamor broke the stillness of the evening, and Charles ended his prayer. The sound of voices came from the marketplace. Truxton couldn't tell if the voices were excited or angry.

The Pilchers rushed from the table to the street front. Clusters of townsfolk were hurrying toward the Capitol, and Truxton heard a single word float out of the confusion . . . *Governor.*

"The Governor, Mother." He turned triumphantly to her. "Did you hear that? He must have decided on a pardon for Father."

Mother pressed forward and joined the crowd at the Capitol building. Truxton followed on her heels.

A burgess whose face he could not see mounted the block by the hitching post and raised his hand for silence. The British officer labored to announce his message.

"This night of October 1770 in the year of our Lord, our beloved Governor Botetourt has died."

The man continued to speak above the hushed murmur of the crowd, but Truxton was stunned. *Governor Botetourt has died.* And with him had died the hope of Father's pardon. Truxton turned and walked as though he slept.

One by one each member of the family returned to the house and then to the table where the dishes still stood.

Mother picked up the small book and read again:

> In chariots some put confidence,
> some horses trust upon:
> But we remember will the name
> of our Lord God alone.

Chapter Twelve
Another Way

Truxton arrived at the gaol in the early morning light. He called out, "Mr. Pelham, I have biscuits for Father."

The heavy door opened slowly, and the gaoler greeted him from within the cell. "Good day, young man. Come—join us."

Truxton stepped into the chamber and heard the door close behind him. Father welcomed him with open arms. "Peter told me about the Governor. We've been talking about the King's law." His voice was steady.

Truxton leaned his head back and looked up into Father's face. Dirty creases lined his forehead, and a rough beard covered his chin.

"I failed."

"Oh, no!" Father hugged him even more tightly. "You are the first Pilcher ever to set foot on royal carpets."

"But . . ."

Father moved his hands to Truxton's shoulders and held him at arm's length. "Our Lord must have another way."

Oh, how Truxton wanted to believe that.

The dimly lit chamber was still. Then Father began to recite. "Psalm 56 verses 3 and 4.

When I'm afraid I'll trust in thee:
In God I'll praise his word;
I will not fear what flesh can do,
my trust is in the Lord."

———————

Truxton was the first to hear the town crier.

"Charles," he whispered.

His brother looked up from his bench and listened intently. The distant call came again. "The judge," he murmured. "He has arrived."

Charles looked at Noble. "Take Elizabeth to the river as Father said."

"Yes, Charles."

No other words were spoken.

Truxton found Mother in the house with her woolen shawl in her hands. Charles laid it across her shoulders, and she tied the ends. "Thank you, Charles."

"Father sent word to bring the Psalter," said Truxton.

"Very well."

Mother breathed deeply and took Charles's arm.

The crowd at the Courthouse parted like soil behind a plow. They allowed the Pilchers to walk directly to a bench behind the rail. Goodrich Scrivner sat at the end of their bench. He leaned forward and lifted his wounded hand.

"Ignore him," whispered Charles.

The bailiff rapped the end of his staff against the floor, and the judge entered the chamber. He wore a fine wig and a handsome suit. Gold-rimmed spectacles rested on his nose.

The dignified man spoke. "I am greatly saddened by the death of Governor Botetourt. As I serve his colony today, I will judge fairly. This was always his desire."

The grievances began. An innkeeper complained that a traveler had not paid for his lodging. The judge asked questions of each. *Please, sir, my Father*. Slowly the judge gave his verdict in this and two other cases.

Finally the bailiff called out, "Mr. Goodrich Scrivner and Mr. Gyles Pilcher, please approach the bench."

Mr. Scrivner stepped through the gate first, then turned to watch as Mr. Pelham brought Father in the rear of the courthouse. People crowded together to let them pass.

The bailiff's loud voice rang out. "Your honor, Gyles Pilcher is charged with purposeful and malicious maiming against the person of Goodrich Scrivner." He added, "Mr. Scrivner asks for the maximum penalty."

The judge looked over the top of his spectacles at Goodrich Scrivner. "I will thank you to allow me to decide."

"Oh, yes, sir. I just want you to consider—"

"Did you hear me, sir?" The judge did not raise his voice nor did the expression on his face change. Mr. Scrivner fell silent. "You have heard the charge against Mr. Pilcher—purposeful and malicious maiming. Is that your claim?"

The large man raised his hand high for all to see. The darkened flesh had begun to grow from one finger to the next. The hand was a scarred mitten. "It is."

The judge looked now at Father. "And how do you answer this charge, Mr. Pilcher?"

Father did not flinch under the man's gaze. "The accident did occur in my foundry, your honor. In the heat of an argument, a crucible of molten pewter spilled on Mr. Scrivner's hand."

"So, Pilcher," Mr. Scrivner called out. "Time in the Public Gaol has cleared your simple mind."

"Silence, sir!"

"Excuse me, your honor." Truxton could hear the mocking sound of Mr. Scrivner's voice.

The room was uncomfortably silent. The judge studied Goodrich Scrivner.

Truxton also looked at the man. He wore a silk waistcoat and satin breeches. His wig was carefully powdered. Truxton looked back at Father. He wore homespun breeches and a soiled shirt. His hair was tied back behind his neck.

The judge spoke again. "Anything more, Mr. Pilcher?"

"Yes, sir." Father's voice filled the courtroom. "I should like to claim the benefit of clergy."

"Claim what?" thundered Mr. Scrivner.

"I am warning you, man." This time the judge raised his voice. "You will have your time to speak, but until then . . . silence!"

Turning back to Father, the judge questioned, "Do you read?"

"I do, sir."

"Do you have a Bible?"

"A Psalter, sir."

"In this room?"

Father's eyes searched for them. Truxton pulled the small volume from his pocket and raised it until Father saw it.

"I do, sir."

"The benefit of clergy . . . 'tis a costly pardon, Mr. Pilcher, for a pewterer." The judge studied Father. "Do you know, sir, that I must record this pardon by branding the brawn of your hand?"

Father turned to look at Peter Pelham, then spoke clearly. "I do, sir."

Truxton looked questioningly at Mother, but she shook her head in ignorance.

The judge turned to Mr. Scrivner. "That your injury is very great I can clearly see. What would you now add to my knowledge of this matter?"

"You can send him to the gallows."

"Have you anything to *add?*"

"Banish him from Williamsburg." Mr. Scrivner demanded. "Close his shop!"

"Mr. Scrivner, under the King's law, Mr. Pilcher has the right to claim the benefit of clergy. He must read before this court the fifty-first Psalm, and then I will restore all his rights as a citizen of this colony." He paused, then asked once more. "Do you wish to share any more about the incident in his foundry?"

Goodrich Scrivner faced the crowd, looking for support, but found none. Finally he answered, "No, your honor."

The judge spoke to Truxton. "The book, please."

Truxton stood and walked to the rail. He placed the small book in Father's hand. His cheeks burned.

"Gyles Pilcher, please read the fifty-first Psalm."

Father read in a strong and steady voice.

> Me cleanse from sin, and throughly wash
> from mine iniquity:
> For my transgressions I confess;
> my sin I ever see.

Verse upon verse, he read. Then Father closed the book.

"I grant to you, Gyles Pilcher of Williamsburg, the benefit of clergy with no further penalty or consequence. From this day forward the mark upon your hand will be our only memory of your crime. The shire reeve will see to the branding."

Chapter Thirteen
Home Again

Truxton stood by the bed. Mother washed Father's branded hand.

"Does it hurt?" asked Elizabeth.

"Of course it does." Mother spoke sharply. She dabbed her cloth on the seared flesh, and Father moaned softly.

"I'm sorry, Gyles." Mother stopped for a moment and covered her eyes with her hand. "I'm almost done."

"Shall I finish for you?" Truxton asked.

Mother looked at the cup of unguent in his hand and nodded. "I would be grateful." She moved aside.

Truxton lifted Father's hand like it was a wounded bird. He smoothed the creamy ointment over the blackened wound.

"Here," whispered Elizabeth. She held out a clean rag.

"Thank you." Truxton took the cloth and handed her the cup. Gently he bound Father's hand, then rested it on a pillow.

"There will be a fearful scar," Truxton said.

" 'Tis the mark of a man," whispered Father, "who claims God's Word."

His eyes closed, and Mother led Truxton and Elizabeth from the room. Father did not leave his bed that day.

In the morning, Father called softly, "Truxton, please come."

Truxton ran to the bed. "Yes, sir?"

"Will you make me a sling?" His voice sounded weak. "I want to get up."

"Here. Take my shawl," said Elizabeth.

Truxton tied it behind Father's neck. He slipped the bandaged hand into the sling and helped Father out of bed.

Father slowly began to walk through the home he had not seen for weeks.

By the time Father's steps brought him to the Foundry, Charles was busy refining a bowl. Noble was readying his mold to accept the fiery molten pewter, and Truxton was tending the bellows at the great fireplace.

"It seems the Pilcher Foundry has suffered little in my absence," said Father.

"Not true!" cried all three. Noble and Charles in turn asked questions of Father and shared concerns that he alone could answer.

Finally Father asked, "And you, Truxton? Have you any questions?"

Truxton looked up from where he knelt. "Yes, sir, I do. But first let me help Noble cast his spoons."

"Very well." Father backed into the corner by the sifting table and watched as the two boys worked. One held the mold steady—the other drew a ladle of molten pewter from the fiery crucible. With great care the ladle was tipped into the mold until the silver liquid mounded gently at the mouth of each spoon. Then the crucible was returned to the hearth.

"You have cast your spoons well, Noble," said Father. "I am very pleased to see all of you tending your duties with care."

Truxton walked from the hearth to Father's bench and dragged the sand mold forward.

Father's eyes were drawn to the scraping sound. "No, son." He shook his head. "I cannot work on the handle." The room was still. "Indeed it will be some time before we will know if this hand *can* finish the work. Put it aside for now and let me hear your question." Father sat on his own stool and with his good hand drew Truxton to his side.

"My question is about your handle, Father. Could I finish repairing it?"

Father turned and studied the mold. A new handle was nearly complete, save the ornament at the top of the curve. He looked at his own bandaged hand. "Can you sketch my handle decoration, Truxton?"

"I think I can, Father, but I have an idea for a shape of my own." Taking up the lead pencil, Truxton began to draw a design etched in his own mind long ago. He sketched it from both sides and then began to draw it from the front. Noble and Charles left their benches and looked over Truxton's shoulder.

Father smiled his approval. "All right, son. Let's pack a small mold and try carving your shape."

With Father's tools, Truxton shaved away the sand until the shape suited his eye, then he mirrored the shape in the other half of the mold. Father directed Truxton's work.

It was late in the day when Father pushed the small mold aside and Truxton moved to the unfinished handle. With great care, the same shape was drawn out of the sand.

Noble and Charles had cleared their benches and gone on to other chores long before Father and Truxton finished their work.

"Will it do?" Truxton looked up into his Father's weary face. Father smiled, and the wrinkles fanned out beside his eyes.

"I should say so." Father stood and stretched. "Tomorrow you and Noble can pour."

Chapter Fourteen
Truxton's Pitcher

The handle came out of the mold like every other handle made in the Pilcher Foundry, but none had ever held Truxton's attention as this one did.

With the utmost patience he filed away the seam made by the mold. He smoothed the lines in the graceful curve of the handle and burnished the piece to a lustrous sheen. After several days of work, it was done. Father asked Charles to weld the handle to the pitcher, and Truxton watched with pride.

"Who will it be for, Father?"

"It was to be sold in Tarpley's Store," Father answered. "But your mother will want to keep it as she did your brothers' first pieces."

That evening the family stood around the simple pine table and turned to look at Father. His hand rested in the sling at his chest. Truxton saw the deep lines etched in Father's face. Surely his hand must hurt.

"Charles, will you read for us?" asked Father. "A short verse tonight. Psalm 63 verse 7, please."

Charles picked up the small book from beside Father's plate. He found the passage and read.

SONGBIRD

> In shadow of thy wings I'll joy;
> for thou mine help hast been.

Father was looking at the new pewter pitcher. "I will think of this verse each time I look at Truxton's pitcher. Only he could have made such a piece."

The small silver pitcher stood by Mother's plate. Perched high on the handle was a shining pewter songbird. The curve of each wing was smooth and strong, and the beak was pointed up to the heavens.

Mother looked long at her son's work, her eyes glistening. Then she raised her gaze to Truxton and smiled. "Truxton Pilcher, I do believe your heart as well as your hands may be suited to birds and bellows alike."

Author's Note

The story told in *Songbird* started long before my pencil ever touched the paper. Just a simple visit to Colonial Williamsburg made me begin to wonder about these people. I started to ask the questions authors ask: who were they, why did they do these things, and what would have happened if . . .?

Truxton and his family came from my imagination, but they represent the hard-working craftsmen who labored in this British colony. I put the Pilchers into the most accurate setting I could create.

PEOPLE

Norbourne Berkeley, the Baron de Botetourt, was the governor of Williamsburg from 1768 to 1770. Governor Botetourt did keep some caged birds in the Governor's Mansion and hoped it was possible for one bird to learn the song of another. He was a bachelor who was well liked by the people of the colony. They were saddened by his sudden death in October of 1770. The records show that he was buried on Friday, October 19.

Peter Pelham was both the gaoler and the organist at the Bruton Parish Church. He sometimes took prisoners with him to services to pump the organ for him. Mr. Pelham did not actually become keeper of the Public Gaol until 1771.

BOOKS

Books were very expensive at this time, so they were owned primarily by the gentry. There were no public libraries as we know them today, just small personal collections. It would not have been unusual for a family like Truxton's to own only one book. If one of the parents could read, he or she would teach the others in the family how to read.

The Catesby book on birds did exist and was considered to be both informative and quite accurate. Descriptions of the Mock-bird and the Tyrant are found in the book.

The Psalter was a small volume that contained just the Book of Psalms written in poetic form or "metre." The passages could be read or sung to certain melodies.

COLONIAL LAW

A person who went to jail was considered guilty and simply awaited the arrival of a judge to give the sentence. The conditions in the jail were crude, with rough straw pallets for beds and little else. Unruly prisoners could be put in shackles and chained to the wall. Food was not necessarily provided by the jailer.

The benefit of clergy was allowed for certain serious crimes. If the person could prove in court the ability to read, he could claim the benefit one time. The fleshy part of the left thumb was branded with an "M" for murder and a "T" for other felonies. This was apparently an old law that came from the time when people who could read were very uncommon and therefore valuable.

I am grateful to Del Moore and Catherine Grosfils at the Colonial Williamsburg Foundation Library and to my friend, Sheila Cribley, for the contributions each made to my research.

n.l.
June 1998

Bibliography

Feduccia, Alan, ed. *Catesby's Birds of Colonial America.* Chapel Hill: University of North Carolina Press, 1985.

Forbes, Esther. *Johnny Tremain.* Boston: Houghton Mifflin, 1971.

Kopper, Philip. *Colonial Williamsburg.* New York: Harry N. Abrams, 1986.

Psalms of David in metre. London: Oxford University Press, n.d.

Rankin, Hugh F. *Criminal Trial Proceedings in the General Court of Colonial Virginia.* Charlottesville: University Press of Virginia, 1965.

San Souci, Robert D. "Apprentice System," *Cobblestone: The History Magazine for Young People,* June 1990, 10-11.

Taylor, Theodore. *Rebellion Town, Williamsburg, 1776.* New York: Thomas Y. Crowell, 1973.

Tripp, Valerie. *An Introduction to Williamsburg.* Middleton, WI: Pleasant Company 1985.

Tunis, Edwin. *Colonial Living.* New York: Thomas Y. Crowell, 1957.

Visiting Our Past: America's Historylands. Washington: National Geographic Society, 1977.